W9-CKT-301

WITHDRAWN

WITHDRAWN

Sleepy Cadillac

Sleepy Cadillac

A BEDTIME DRIVE

BY THACHER HURD

HARPERCOLLINS*PUBLISHERS*

3 1267 13898 4602

To Olivia
—T.H.

Sleepy Cadillac: A Bedtime Drive
Copyright © 2005 by Thacher Hurd

Manufactured in China by South China Printing Company Ltd.

All rights reserved. No part of this book may be used or reproduced in any manner whatsoever without written permission
except in the case of brief quotations embodied in critical articles and reviews. For information address HarperCollins
Children's Books, a division of HarperCollins Publishers, 1350 Avenue of the Americas, New York, NY 10019.
www.harperchildrens.com

Library of Congress Cataloging-in-Publications Data
Hurd, Thacher.
Sleepy Cadillac : a bedtime drive / by Thacher Hurd.— 1st ed.
p. cm.
Summary: A nighttime ride in the Sleepy Cadillac ensures every passenger a night of happy dreams and cozy sleep.
ISBN 0-06-073020-X — ISBN 0-06-073021-8 (lib. bdg.)
[1. Bedtime—Fiction. 2. Sleep—Fiction.] I. Title.
PZ7.H9562Sl 2005
[E]—dc22   2004007826
                                                                                         CIP
                                                                                         AC

Typography by Al Cetta   1 2 3 4 5 6 7 8 9 10   ❖   First Edition
The illustrations were done in pastels and pastel pencils.

The sun is going down.
The Sleepy Cadillac is floating
down the street.

The Sleepy Cadillac stops
by your window.
Climb aboard.

The Sleepy Cadillac is big and blue,
and the seats are soft.
Snuggle in.

The steering wheel turns.
The tires hum.
The engine purrs.

"Beep" goes the horn.
"Shhhhhh" the air flows by.
The Sleepy Cadillac is going
for a drive.

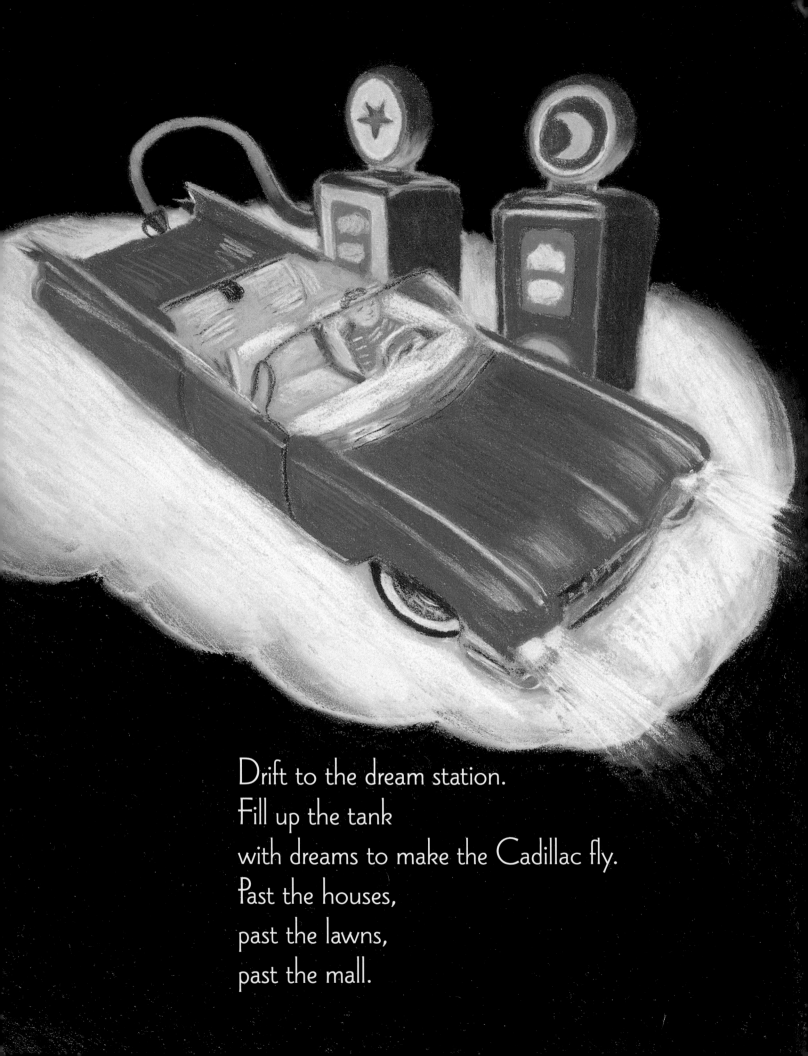

Drift to the dream station.
Fill up the tank
with dreams to make the Cadillac fly.
Past the houses,
past the lawns,
past the mall.

Down a winding road
and into the fog.
The dashboard glows.
The headlights shine
through the night,
through the fog.

Now the Sleepy Cadillac floats
above the fog.
Over the trees.
Over the houses.
Over all the wide, green country.

Look up.
The stars light the way.
The moon lights the way.

Over the ocean,
where the whales are sleeping,
the waves are gently rolling,
and the dolphins sing
a sleepy song
in the deep blue sea.

Up and up goes the Sleepy Cadillac,
until it is high above the ocean,
high above the clouds,
close to the moon.

Look behind.
The rest of the sleepy cars are following.

All the way to Pajama Land.
Big moon,
laughing in the sky,
shows the way.

Sleepy cars circle the moon,
dance in the light
round and round.

Until all the eyes droop
and all the heads nod,
and everyone dreams the night away.

Then all around the world one more time.

The Sleepy Cadillac floats down,
down to your window.

And you climb into bed,
soft and warm
all around.